Instant Poetry Frames
for Primary Poets

by Betsy Franco

SCHOLASTIC
PROFESSIONAL BOOKS

New York • Toronto • London • Auckland • Sydney • Mexico City • New Delhi • Hong Kong • Buenos Aires

For the children in Denise Dauler's classes,
who give me ideas every day.

Cover design by Norma Ortiz

Cover and interior illustrations by Maxie Chambliss

Interior design by Ellen Matlach Hassell
for Boultinghouse & Boultinghouse, Inc.

ISBN: 0-439-30363-X

Contents

Poetry Frames

Introduction

Imagine the satisfaction budding young poets will feel when they write their very own poem or collection of poems! With the help of the simple frames and structures in this book, children can write an entire "anthology" on their own—and quickly experience writing success.

What Are Poetry Frames?

Poetry frames are quick and easy reproducible "invitations" into the world of poetry. They are structures that provide inspiration for children to create their own poems—while providing the scaffolding young writers need. Art on each page serves as a visual cue, and space is often provided for children to illustrate their own poetry.

Why Use Poetry Frames?

To build writing skills and meet the language arts standards.
Confident writers are more able writers. With these frames, children develop a range of writing skills that will bolster confidence and the desire to write more! They will:

- write in a variety of poetry genres
- organize their ideas
- sequence events
- use pictures to describe text
- focus on specific parts of speech
- apply mechanical conventions to their writing
- write for a variety of purposes (to entertain, inform, explain, and describe)
- edit and "publish" their work
- use prewriting strategies to plan written work
- **and much more!**

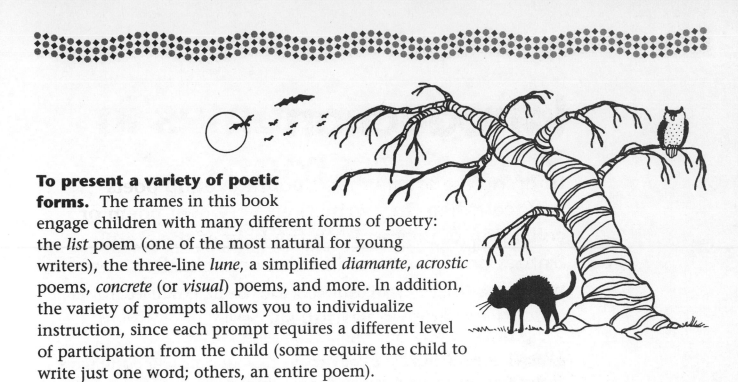

To present a variety of poetic forms. The frames in this book engage children with many different forms of poetry: the *list* poem (one of the most natural for young writers), the three-line *lune*, a simplified *diamante*, *acrostic* poems, *concrete* (or *visual*) poems, and more. In addition, the variety of prompts allows you to individualize instruction, since each prompt requires a different level of participation from the child (some require the child to write just one word; others, an entire poem).

To encourage self-expression. Thought-provoking poetry frames help children reveal personal preferences and different aspects of their world. They write about their hopes and dreams, their strengths and challenges, and the ways they are growing. The prompts spark imagination and encourage children's natural playfulness!

To introduce the basic elements of poetry. Children are introduced to similes, metaphors, personification, alliteration, and more. They are encouraged to use poetic language and interesting imagery. Children also play with specific parts of speech: naming words (nouns), action words (verbs), and describing words (adjectives).

To build awareness of rhyme and repetition. The poems have a sense of rhythm and repetition that make them fun to write and to read aloud. Often, a fun rhyme is provided as the final couplet, enabling children to write freely and still have a structured rhyming poem when they finish. Other times, they are given a set of rhyming words to create a poem, or to supply the final rhyming word. In addition, many of the poems have repeating patterns that scaffold children's writing.

To integrate math and science into your language arts curriculum. Math and science need not take a backseat in the poetry world! Children count their shoelace holes, the zippers on their backpacks, and more as they complete the poem "Counting on Me." In "Faster than a Snail," they compare the heights, lengths, and speeds of different animals.

Using the Frames in Your Classroom

Each poem can be written individually, with partners, or as a class collaboration. Here's how you might use the frames with children:

1. Copy the frame of your choice for each child. Introduce the frame with the group before children begin. Review the directions together and write an example as a class.

2. Provide children with a copy of the reproducible frame and have them use pencil and crayons or markers.

3. Circulate around the room to check that each child is engaged, helping to brainstorm when needed.

After poems are completed, celebrate kids' efforts by inviting them to:

- share with a partner or a small group
- read to the class or to an older buddy
- copy their poem onto a blank sheet of paper and illustrate as part of a display.
- make into a class collaborative book for the classroom library
- display on bulletin boards
- take home and share with families
- make them into pocket chart strips (children's versions of a poem can be written on blank strips and then displayed and chanted by the class)
- act out the poems
- create their very own anthology by binding all their poems together!
- hold a poetry reading in which each child reads his or her poem to the whole class.

Instant Poetry Frames
for Primary Poets

Write on each blank line to create a poem about your shadow.
Then draw a picture of you and your shadow.

My Shadow

My shadow is a special friend.
It copies what I do.

If I _____,
my shadow does it, too.

If I _____,
my shadow sticks like glue.

Whatever I do on sunny days,
my shadow likes to do!

by _____

Me and My Shadow

Instant Poetry Frames for Primary Poets   Scholastic Professional Books

Finish this poem about your backpack.
Use the words in the box to help you get started:

heavy	clean	old	pockets
light	dirty	new	zippers

My Backpack

My backpack is _____.

My backpack has _____.

It's _____. That's a color that's cool.

Inside it I carry my _____

and my _____.

And it rides on me all the way to school!

by _____

Write about the things that someone would see in your bedroom.
Include special things that say something about you.

In My Room

If you look in my room,

here's what you'll see:

_____,

_____,

and _____.

_____,

_____,

and _____.

If you look in my room,

that's what you'll see.

My room can tell you lots about me!

by _____

Instant Poetry Frames for Primary Poets Scholastic Professional Books

What do you hope will happen someday? Write about it. Then draw a picture of one of your wishes coming true.

Someday

Someday I hope _____

_____

Someday I hope _____

_____

Someday I hope _____

_____

If I do everything that I can do,
someday my wishes just might come true.

by _____

This kind of poem is called a *lune*.
Each line has a certain number of words.

Tiny sow bug   (3 words)
curled up in my hand—   (5 words)
scared, cozy, round.   (3 words)

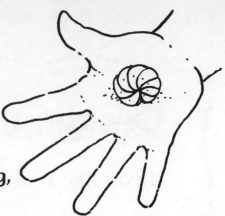

Now write your own lune about a spider, ladybug, firefly, or another bug. Then illustrate your lune.

Lune Bug

_____   (3 words)

_____   (5 words)

_____   (3 words)

by _____

Instant Poetry Frames for Primary Poets Scholastic Professional Books

Here's a silly poem for you to finish.

Deciding What Pet to Get

If you like barking,

get a _____.

If you like _____,

get a _____.

If you like _____,

_____.

If you like _____,

_____.

But if you like it quiet,

then get a fish.

It swims around with

a quiet "swish."

by _____

Instant Poetry Frames for Primary Poets   Scholastic Professional Books

Write a poem about a thunder and lightning storm.
You can use these questions to help get you started:

- What do you hear?
- What do you see?
- How do you feel?
- What do you do?

The Storm

_____

_____

_____

_____

_____

_____

_____

_____

_____

by _____

Instant Poetry Frames for Primary Poets   Scholastic Professional Books

Fill in the blanks with things you like to do at recess.
Save your favorite activity for last!
Then draw yourself on the playground doing what you like to do best.

At Recess

At recess,

I like to _____.

I like to _____.

So those are the things I often play.

But my favorite thing to do is

_____

so I do it almost every day!

by _____

Instant Poetry Frames for Primary Poets   Scholastic Professional Books

Write about when you were small and what you're like now.
(Think about what you liked to do, what you looked like, what you were scared of,
what you wore, and your favorite toys.)
Then draw two pictures, one of yourself when you were small and one of you now.

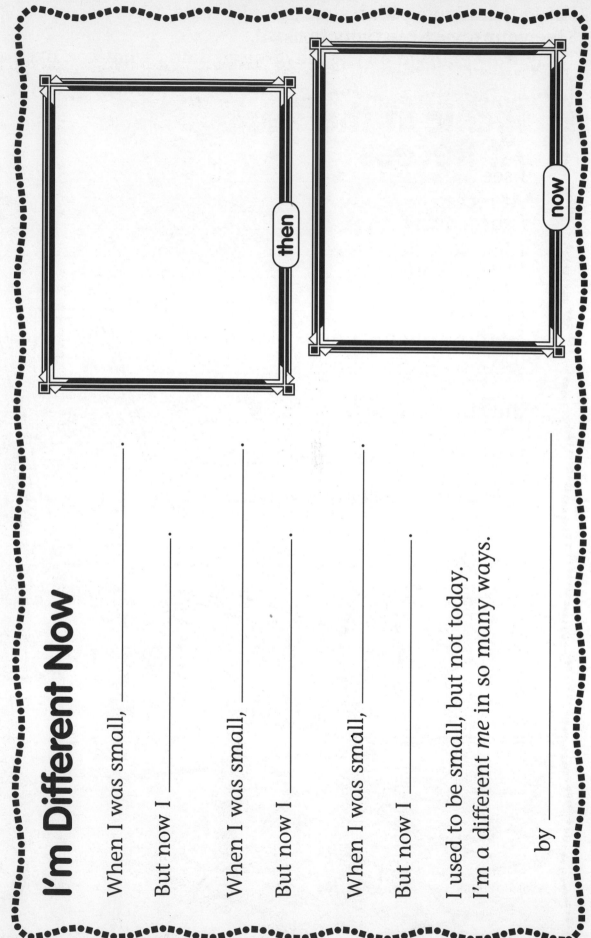

then

now

I'm Different Now

When I was small, _____

But now I _____

When I was small, _____

But now I _____

When I was small, _____

But now I _____

I used to be small, but not today.
I'm a different *me* in so many ways.

by _____

Instant Poetry Frames for Primary Poets   Scholastic Professional Books

Finish this picnic poem.
The pictures can give you ideas.

Picnic in the Park

I see _____.

I shoo away _____.

I munch on _____.

I eat lots of _____.

We play _____.

We play _____.

Darn—it's time to leave the park,

because it's really getting dark!

by _____

What things are hard for you? What things are easy? Write about them in the poem.

Hard and Easy

Its hard to _____

but it's easy to _____

Its hard to _____

but it's easy to _____

Some things are easy, some are hard, some are in between.

Some things are hard 'cause I'm _____ years old.

They'll be easy when I'm seventeen!

by _____

hard   easy

Instant Poetry Frames for Primary Poets   Scholastic Professional Books

Write a poem about the four seasons.
Use words that paint a picture, like:

Fall is bright colors twirling through the sky.

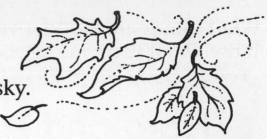

All Year Round

Fall is crunching leaves on the walk to school.

Fall is _____.

Winter is _____.

Winter is _____.

Spring is _____.

Spring is _____.

Summer is _____.

Summer is _____.

Winter, spring, summer, fall.

_____'s my favorite season of all.

by _____

   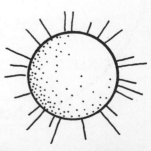

What do you think animals dream about?
Fill in the blanks.

Animal Dreams

Do horses dream of having horns?

Do mice dream of being big?

Do sheep have dreams of _____?

Does _____ fill the dreams of pigs?

Do cows dream of _____?

Do goats dream of being kings?

Do frogs dream of _____?

Do dogs dream of having wings?

Chickens dream about _____.

Roosters dream they can talk and shout.

I've dreamed about _____.

Dreams are weird—there is no doubt!

by _____

Instant Poetry Frames for Primary Poets   Scholastic Professional Books

Write opposites in the blanks.
You can use the words in the box to
help you, or use words of your own.

clean	white	cute
mean	thin	night

Opposite Cats

_____Big_____ cats,

_____Small_____ cats,

Like-to-play-with-yarn cats.

_____ cats,

_____ cats,

Sleep-all-day-and-yawn cats.

_____ cats,

_____ cats,

Chased-by-neighbor's-dog cats.

_____ cats,

_____ cats,

Curl-up-in-your-bed cats.

by _____

Instant Poetry Frames for Primary Poets   Scholastic Professional Books

Pick a topic from this list:

a baseball game	the beach
Thanksgiving	the forest
Halloween	a carnival
lunchtime at school	your backyard
your neighborhood	your favorite restaurant

Write about what you hear, see, smell, taste, and touch.
Then draw what you see.

My Five Senses

I hear _____.

I see _____.

I smell _____.

I taste _____.

I touch _____.

by _____

Instant Poetry Frames for Primary Poets   Scholastic Professional Books

Write about an imaginary animal. The words in the box can help you get started.

Then draw your animal!

beak	horns	scales
tail	fur	stinger
wings	paws	antennae
fangs	fins	whiskers

My Imaginary Animal

My animal has _____ on its _____,

and _____ on its toes.

It has _____ on its _____

And _____ near its nose.

It has special _____ on its head.

It's scared of _____,

and it sleeps all day under my bed!

by _____

Use the picture to help you fill in the blanks.

Alone or Together

I can _____ all by myself.

But it takes two to _____.

Two or three can _____.

But it takes more to _____.

With lots of kids, you can _____.

We play that game sometimes at school.

But I can _____ all by myself

and that's also pretty cool!

by _____

Instant Poetry Frames for Primary Poets   Scholastic Professional Books

Instant Poetry Frames for Primary Poets Scholastic Professional Books

Fill in the blanks to finish this animal poem.

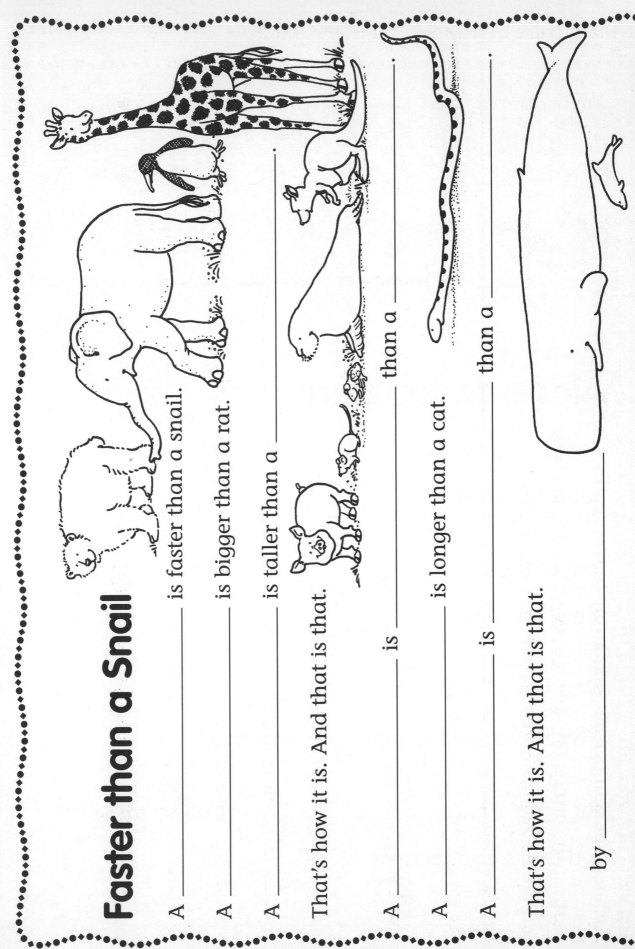

Faster than a Snail

A ——————— is faster than a snail.

A ——————— is bigger than a rat.

A ——————— is taller than a ———————.

That's how it is. And that is that.

A ——————— is ——————— than a ———————.

A ——————— is longer than a cat.

A ——————— is ——————— than a ———————.

That's how it is. And that is that.

by ———————

26

Write about your grandfather, grandmother, or another relative using similes.
First write the word *his* or *her* in the first blank on each line of the poem.
Then describe that person, comparing him or her to something else, like:

EXAMPLE: <u>His hands are like <u>leaves baked by the sun.</u></u>

Now draw a picture of the person you picked.

My _____

_____ hands are like _____

_____ hair is like _____

_____ face is like _____

_____ voice is like _____

_____ smile is like _____

by _____

Finish this poem about a pet shop. Use interesting words!

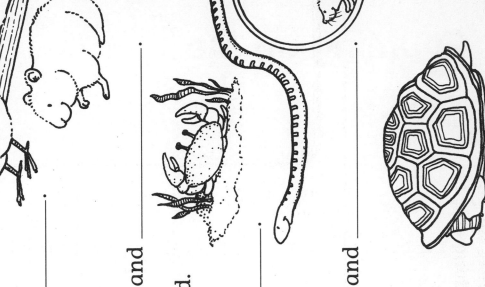

The Pet Shop

The parakeet is _____ and _____ .

The hamster is fluffy and cuddles up in my hand.

The _____ is _____ and _____ .

The crab in the fish tank burrows down in the sand.

The snake is _____ and _____ .

The mouse rides his wheel and goes for a ride.

The _____ is _____ and _____ .

But the turtle always hides inside!

by _____

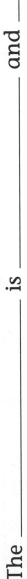

Instant Poetry Frames for Primary Poets   Scholastic Professional Books

Count things to complete this poem!
Then draw yourself.
Show some of the things you counted in the poem.

Counting on Me

I have _____ pockets,

_____ shoelace holes,

_____ big wrinkles on my thumb,

_____ long lines on the palm of my hand,

and _____ great big smile

that goes on for a mile.

      by _____

Instant Poetry Frames for Primary Poets   Scholastic Professional Books

Write about a stuffed animal!
Write the word *His* or *Her* in the first blank on each line.
Then compare the animal's body parts to something else.

EXAMPLE: <u>His</u> eyes are like <u>two shiny black beetles</u>.

Then draw your stuffed animal sitting on your bed.

My Stuffed Animal

_____ eyes are like _____.

_____ ears are like _____.

_____ nose is like _____.

_____ feet are like _____.

_____ fur is like _____.

And every night it sleeps with me

and always keeps me company.

by _____

Use these rhyming words to write a scary poem about Halloween. Rhyme every two lines.

fright	ghost	bat	sky	boo
night	most	hat	fly	goo
bright	boast	cat	why	do
sight	almost	that	eye	who
white			high	grew
			nearby	too
			good-bye	
			you and I	

Halloween Night

It's Halloween night.
The moon is round and bright.

_____

_____

_____

_____

_____

by _____

Instant Poetry Frames for Primary Poets Scholastic Professional Books

Write a round poem! Pretend you are one of these round things:

yo-yo	balloon	cake	soccer ball
clock	pizza	gum ball	bubble

Use these questions to help you write your poem.

- **What would you look like?**
- **How would you move?**
- **What would you be good at?**

- **What would you spend time doing?**
- **What would people do with you?**
- **How would you feel?**

If I were a _____,

I'd _____

_____

I'd _____

_____

I'd _____

_____

If I were a _____.

by _____

Instant Poetry Frames for Primary Poets   Scholastic Professional Books

Read this animal-sound poem out loud.
Don't be afraid to have fun and get silly!

The Little Green Frog

Gla-goong went the little green frog one day.
Gla-goong went the little green frog.
Gla-goong went the little green frog one day.
And his eyes went *gla, gla, goong.*

Now pick an animal from this list, or
use any other animal.

donkey	duck	goose	pony
sheep	mouse	pig	

Make up a new sound for your animal!

The Little

_____ _____ went the little _____ one day.

_____ went the little _____.

_____ _____ went the little _____ one day.

And his _____ went _____

by _____ .

Instant Poetry Frames for Primary Poets   Scholastic Professional Books

To make a silly scramble poem:

1. Cut out the words at right.
2. Turn them over and mix them up.
3. Pick one short strip and one long strip.
4. Write the two words you picked on each of the dotted blanks.
5. Fill in the rest of the blanks in the poem.

EXAMPLE:

A lollipop growls
when you eat it too fast.

growls	hiccups	cries	honks
spider	sock	lollipop	ladybug

Silly Scramble

A ....

when ....

A ....

when ....

A ....

when ....

When a ....
we all come to hear.
We all come to hear it
from far and from near!

by ....

Write a "poem for your pocket" below!
In your poem, list what kinds of things come in kids' pockets:

• **What kinds of things to eat?**
• **What kinds of toys?**
• **What kinds of money?**
• **What other things?**

Kids' Pockets

Kids have lots of things inside their pockets:

_____

_____

_____

_____

_____

_____

_____

What's inside yours?

by _____

Instant Poetry Frames for Primary Poets Scholastic Professional Books

Write a "sound effects" poem!
Here's an example:

Train Ride
"All abooooard!"
klang, kling
charooga, charooga
chooooo, chooooo
krickety-klack
down the track.

Write a sound effects poem of
your own. Pick one of these ideas:

- recess
- airport
- nighttime
- school bus ride
- jungle
- drum practice

Write the sounds you would hear.
Make up words if you want!

_____

_____

_____

_____

_____

_____

_____

by _____

Write a poem-letter to a type of weather, like:

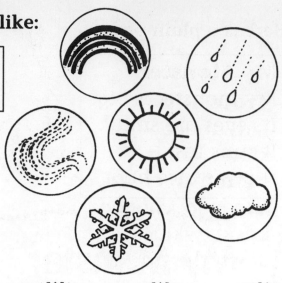

clouds	wind	rain	sunshine
storm	fog	snow	rainbow

On each line, you might:
- tell it something
- ask it a question
- complain about it
- say something nice about it
- tell it what you would like it to do

Dear _____,

_____

_____

_____

_____

_____

_____

Yours truly,

_____

by _____

Instant Poetry Frames for Primary Poets   Scholastic Professional Books

Here is a plain poem:

Fill in the blanks to write the same poem in a more interesting way. Then draw a picture of your monster.

> **My Monster**
> My monster is big.
> Its eyes are small.
> It runs fast.
> It gives nice hugs.

My Monster

My monster is as enormous as _____.

When it goes gallumphing across the playground, it looks

like _____.

But its hugs are so warm and cozy, they feel like

_____!

My monster is rather strange to see,

but it's always a very good friend to me!

by _____

These lines show how a snake moves. Tell how it feels
to be along for the ride by writing on the lines!

Slithering with a Snake

When I ride on the back of a snake,

by _____

Instant Poetry Frames for Primary Poets Scholastic Professional Books

You can write a riddle poem.
Pick an object from this list or think of your own:

scooter	television	basketball	swimming pool
kite	ice skates	bicycle	rollerblades

Tell how to use it.

EXAMPLE:

Drag it up the hill.
Jump on, tummy first.
Whooosh through the snow!
Get snow dust in your face.
Tumble off.
Drag it back up the hill!
What is it? _____sled_____

Now write your own riddle poem
and give it to a friend to answer!

Riddle Poem

_____

_____

_____

_____

_____

What is it? _____

by _____

What if the foods at the supermarket come alive when the store closes at night? Finish the poem by telling what different foods might do.

Midnight in the Supermarket

The broccoli was scared of the dark.
The oranges rolled up and down the aisles.
The turkey waltzed with the hamburger meat.

The cookies _____.

The orange juice _____.

The popcorn _____.

The carrots _____.

The pretzels _____.

But when the store opened up,
they jumped back on the shelves,
and they acted just like
their everyday selves!

by _____

Instant Poetry Frames for Primary Poets Scholastic Professional Books

When you compare two things that are different, you are making a *metaphor*. Tell what color each feeling is and why you think so.
Then decorate this page with all of the colors you wrote about!

A Rainbow of Feelings

 Excited is the color _____

because when I get excited _____.

 Angry is the color _____

because _____.

 Sad is the color _____

because _____.

 Happy is the color _____

because _____.

Everyone has a whole rainbow of feelings!

by _____

Instant Poetry Frames for Primary Poets   Scholastic Professional Books

To write a squiggle poem, first make a squiggle above the poem.
Write a poem about your squiggle.
What does it look like? What is happening in your squiggle?

My Squiggle

My squiggle _____

_____.

My squiggle _____

_____.

My squiggle _____

_____.

I see lots of things in my very own squiggle

that twists and turns and curves and wiggles.

by _____

Instant Poetry Frames for Primary Poets   Scholastic Professional Books

Write about "The Purple Plane" or "The Bright Blue Bus."

If you write about the purple plane, use as many P words as you can.

If you write about the bright blue bus, use as many B words as you can.

To get started, think about these things:

- What kinds of animals are riding in the plane or the bus?
- Where are they going?
- What are they eating?
- What are they doing?
- What do they see out the window?

Draw a picture of your plane or bus.

_____

_____

_____

_____

_____

by _____

Write a poem about some jobs you might like to have.
Then draw a picture of you doing one of the jobs.

Any Job at All

If I could have any job at all,

I'd be a _____

because _____.

Or I'd be a _____

because _____.

Or I'd be a _____

because _____.

If I could have any job at all,
I'd take one I love and I'd have a ball!

      by _____

Instant Poetry Frames for Primary Poets   Scholastic Professional Books

To write a diamante poem, first pick one of these topics or think of your own:

bunny	snow	chocolate
kite	puppy	grasshopper
	seed	pizza

Write the topic word on the first line of the poem.
Write it again on the last line of the poem.
Your poem will look like a diamond if you write only on the lines.

Diamante Poem

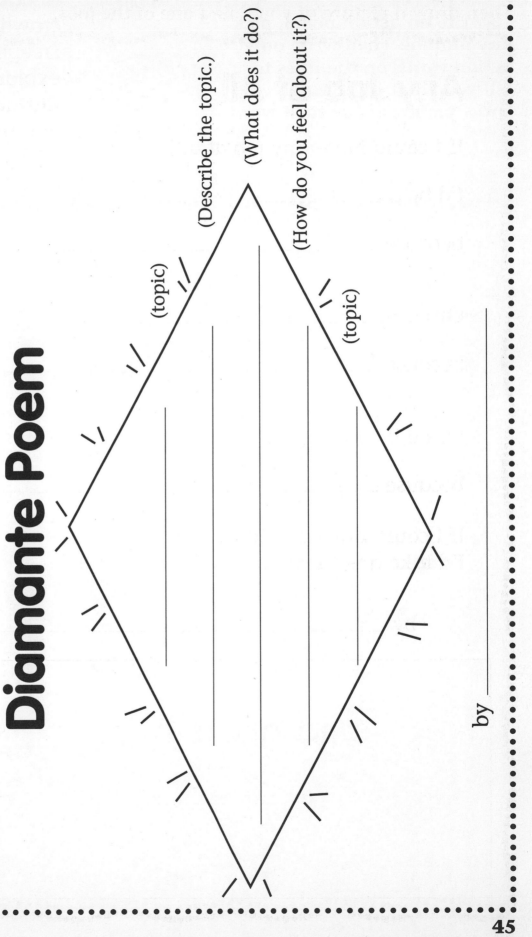

(topic)

(Describe the topic.)

(What does it do?)

(How do you feel about it?)

(topic)

by _____

Action!

To write an action poem, pick any animal. Then write only action words on the lines to tell you what it is doing! Draw pictures near each word.

EXAMPLE:

A Ladybug on Me
crawling
creeping
exploring
flitting
flying
and good-bying!

_____

_____ing

_____ing

_____ing

_____ing

_____ing

and good-bying!

by _____

Instant Poetry Frames for Primary Poets Scholastic Professional Books

An acrostic poem uses certain letters to start off each line.
This is an acrostic poem that uses the name Joey:

Name Poem
Just a great kid
Only child
Everybody knows he loves soccer
Yes, he's a good friend.

Now write your own acrostic poem using
your own name or a friend's name.

Name Poem

_____

_____

_____

_____

_____

_____

_____

_____

by _____

Notes